Destiny's
IN LOVE

Look for these and other books about Linelle Destiny in the Linelle Destiny Series:

Visit www.thesecretsistersclub.com

Linelle Destiny Series

Destiny's IN LOVE

Dr. Alicia Holland

Illustrations by Anoop PC

This book may be ordered through booksellers or by contacting:

iGlobal Educational Services, LLC
13785 Highway 183, Suite 125
Austin, Texas 78750
www.iglobaleducation.com
512-761-5898

Because of the dynamic nature of the Internet, any web addresses or links contained in this book may have changed since publication and may no longer be valid. The views expressed in this work are solely those of the author and do not necessarily reflect the views of the publisher, and the publisher hereby disclaims any responsibility for them.

This is a work of fiction. Names, characters, businesses, places, events, and incidents are either the products of the author's imagination or used in a fictitious manner. Any resemblance to actual persons, living or dead, or actual events is purely coincidental.

Linelle Destiny Series: Destiny's in Love

ISBN-13: 978-1-944346-07-2

Acknowledgements

I want to first honor God for placing in my heart to share my story with others. It was He whom brought Karen and I together to manifest this project. I am so grateful for Karen Hendry as she took my notes and helped write this fictitious book. There are truly no words to express my gratitude as you are truly a blessing.

I also want to thank Surendra Gupta for his creativity in formatting and Anoop PC for his creativity in bringing life to the designs and illustrations in this book series. Both of you are amazing!

Dedication

I dedicate this book series to my beautiful and talented daughters, Georgia and Amaiya Johnson. Remember, you are valued, loved, and competent. You are worthy!

Part 1
Summer Program

Chapter 1
After Graduation

The graduation ceremony is over and Destiny thinks everything is all wrapped up, but when they arrive home she is surprised to find that her family has planned a surprise party for her. Everything has been set out. There are balloons and decorations and a big cake. When Destiny looks closely at the cake she sees that it has her picture on it and it says "Congratulations Linelle Destiny Sycamores!"

"Wow, thank you everyone!" says Destiny when everyone arrives. Her brothers, Keith and Dino, are there; her sister, Michelle; her aunts and uncles; and of course Momma and Pop.

"Honey," says Destiny's Pop as he bends down and gives her a kiss, "You deserve it."

"You sure do, child," says Momma. "I am so proud of you, sugar. You have done us mighty proud." Momma gives Destiny a big hug and everyone else hugs her and tells her how proud they are of her.

Michelle is the last to come up to Destiny. "I can't believe I used to change your diapers, little sister," she says, giving Destiny a hug. "Now you're all grown up."

"Thanks, Michelle," says Destiny.

"And you know what the best part is?" asked Michelle.

"What?" asked Destiny.

"We will be able to go to school together, now!"

Michelle is enrolled at Northwestern State University as a part-time student. It's the school Destiny chose to enrol in, to stay close to home.

"Yes!" says Destiny. She has never attended school with her siblings because she is so much younger than they are. "We can carpool and study together and meet for lunch."

"It will be wonderful," says Michelle. "Now, I need to get some of that good-smelling food!" Michelle saunters off to the food table.

Destiny is grateful to her family for throwing her a party. It is such a nice surprise and it's almost perfect. But one thing is missing.

Destiny goes over to Momma and says, "This party is perfect, Momma. The only thing missing is my friends."

"I did invite them, child. Talked to their mammas myself, but they couldn't come. I guess they were busy with something else."

"Thanks for trying, Momma," says Destiny, but she has a feeling her friends weren't busy. They just didn't want to come.

It is a couple of days after graduation and Destiny is working a shift at the grocery store. Coming back from her break,

Destiny sees Barbara down one of the aisles. She walks over and says, "Hi Barbara."

Barbara looks at Destiny and says, "Oh, hi. I didn't know you were still working here." Destiny thinks Barbara sounds distant.

"Yes, I still work here," says Destiny. "How are you? I was hoping to see you at the graduation party my parents threw for me."

"Yeah, well, I was busy," says Barbara, not looking at Destiny.

"Oh, right. I see," says Destiny turning away. "Well, see ya."

As Destiny is walking back down the aisle, Barbara says, "Destiny, wait."

Destiny stops and turns around.

"I am proud of you," says Barbara. "I just know that you're leaving us. There isn't any point in pretending otherwise."

With that, Barbara turns and walks away.

Destiny goes back to her cash register and gets ready to open up. But she feels so sad that she just stands there for a minute, trying to fight back the tears that are threatening to pour down her cheeks.

"Hey, are you okay?"

Destiny looks up to see Calix. "Yeah, I'm fine," she says.

"I can see you're upset about something," says Calix.

"No, it's okay," says Destiny. "Really. Just saying goodbye to an old friend."

"Goodbye? But you're not going anywhere, are you?"

"No, but I graduated early and I'm going to college next year and she's not," says Destiny. "She feels left behind and doesn't want to be friends anymore."

"I'm sorry, Destiny," says Calix.

"That's okay," Destiny replies, perking up. "I'm starting a whole new adventure this summer and I'm sure I'll meet new friends." She didn't add that no one could replace Barbara.

"Well, I hope you don't go meeting new guys, too," says Calix.

Destiny suddenly feels hot in the face. "I don't have time for that," she says, getting ready to open her cash register. "I have to focus on my books."

Calix considers Destiny with a serious look in his eyes. "That's good," he says, "because I'm crazy about you and one day I'm gonna marry you."

"Oh my, Calix," says Destiny, stunned by the determination in his voice. "I'm flattered, but like I said, I'm focused on my books right now." *And I'm nowhere near ready to think about marriage*, she thinks.

"That's just fine," says Calix. "I can wait. I'm a patient man." And with that, Calix is gone, leaving Destiny standing there with a lineup starting to form at her cash register.

Chapter 2
Summer Session

It's the first day of classes and Destiny can hardly contain her excitement. She is finally and truly a college girl. She pulls up at Michelle's house and she doesn't have to wait long before Michelle comes out and hops in the car.

Destiny's nephews Carlos, Alex, and Junior are at the door waving goodbye to Michelle. They see Destiny and wave at her, too. Destiny waves back and the kids disappear into the house.

"They're getting so big," says Destiny. She doesn't get to see them very often because she is so busy with school and work all the time.

"Yes, they are," says Michelle, "and they miss their Aunt Nene."

"I'll have to come see them soon," Destiny replies, backing out of Michelle's driveway.

"All ready for your first day?" asks Michelle, clutching her travel mug full of coffee and placing her backpack by her feet.

"You bet I am," says Destiny. "College Algebra, here I come!" The truth was, Destiny really wanted to get Math, English, and

Science over with as quickly as possible, so she elected to take College Algebra, Literature, and Chemistry during her summer session.

After her summer program at Louisiana Tech, Destiny realized she didn't want to be a nurse. Her heart lay in teaching, plain and simple. Now Destiny is enrolled in the Teacher Education program and following her passion.

"What are you looking forward to the most?" asks Michelle. "And I know you're not going to say the college boys."

"What?" says Destiny, "Who says I don't like boys?"

"No one said it," says Michelle, "but I don't think you're going to look up from your books long enough to notice any boys."

"Very funny," says Destiny. "As for what I'm looking forward to the most. Everything! All of it! I don't think I can pick just one."

"That's my little sister," says Michelle, as they pull into the college parking lot. "You never think small, do you?"

Destiny shakes her head as she parks the car.

"As for me," says Michelle, "I'm looking forward to getting another coffee and being away from the kids for a few hours."

Later that day, after classes are over, Destiny is working on her math homework when her Momma calls in to her. "Destiny, honey. Would you please run to the store and pick up a few things for me?"

Destiny comes out of her room. "Sure, Momma. What do you need?"

"Here's a list, child," says Momma, handing Destiny a piece of paper. "Pop parked behind you so you'll have to take his truck.

He wants you to put gas in it while you're out, anyway." Momma hands Destiny some money. "This should cover everything."

"Okay, Momma," says Destiny, kissing Momma on the cheek. "I'll be back soon."

Destiny goes to the gas station first, the big one up on the hill. When Destiny gets out of the truck, a young man walks up to her and says, "What's a beautiful, short girl like you getting out a big truck like that?"

Destiny's Pop drives a great big white Ford 4x4 pickup truck. Everyone around town knows it's Pop's truck and he loves it. Destiny answers the young man, "I like big things." She notices how handsome he is, with his nice clothes and big brown eyes. He certainly is very well dressed.

The man just smiles at her and walks away. Destiny sighs and gases up her Pop's truck. She wishes she would have gotten the man's name. Oh well, she hasn't got time to date anyone anyway. Isn't that what she told Calix?

Later that evening, when Destiny is back in her room study-ing, she has a vision. She can see it. The Secret Sisters Club isn't finished after all. Despite the fact that the two friends who started it with her are no longer in her life, Kendall having moved away three years ago and Barbara choosing not to be friends with her anymore, her vision shows her that the Secret Sisters Club really is alive and well. In fact, it has grown bigger and better.

Destiny sees girls holding meetings in different countries around the world. She sees them raising money to support a number of causes, making a true difference in the world and learning important leadership skills along the way. She sees herself speaking with girls in France, England, Australia, Canada, and Jamaica. It is truly wonderful!

When the vision ends, Destiny sits in silence for a few minutes, completely in awe of what she has seen. When she first came up with the idea for the Secret Sisters Club she had no idea it would become anything more than a club for local girls, although she definitely wanted it to be more, to make a bigger impact.

Destiny knows with absolute certainty that she has to do what it takes to make the vision become a reality and she needs to start by focusing on her books like never before. She will also need money to get the bigger version of the Secret Sisters Club off the ground and she vows to save up all of her work money to help make it happen.

Destiny smiles to herself. The knowledge that she will make such a difference in the lives of so many girls around the world is such as amazing and comforting thought. Life has a lot in store for her and Destiny is ready to make it happen!

But first I need to get this algebra homework done, Destiny thinks as she turns her attention back to the work in front of her.

Chapter 3
Jalaney

Acouple of weeks into summer classes, Destiny is walking to Algebra class with Michelle. "So, Destiny," says Michelle, "I have some news to tell you."

"Really?" asks Destiny. "What?"

"You're going to be an aunty again."

"What? Seriously?" says Destiny.

"Yeah," says Michelle. "I just found out yesterday. Number four is on its way." She smiles and pats her stomach. "I hope it's a girl this time. I love my boys, but I'd really like a daughter, too. You know?"

Michelle walks into the classroom, leaving Destiny stunned and scrambling to catch up. She is so distracted that she bumps into a boy who is going through the door at the same time. Destiny drops her books and he bends down to help her pick them up.

"So sorry," he says.

"No, it's okay," says Destiny. "I wasn't paying attention to where I was going."

The boy holds out his hand when they stand up, "I'm Jalaney," he says, introducing himself.

"I'm Destiny," says Destiny shaking his hand.

Destiny sits next to Michelle and Jalaney sits next to Destiny.

"I really don't like this class," says Jalaney. "I'm here on a football scholarship and if anything is gonna drag down my marks it's gonna be math."

"Football?" says Destiny. "That sounds exciting."

"Do you do any sports?" asks Jalaney.

"I used to run track, but I wasn't good enough to get in on a scholarship. At least, not for my sports skills."

"You here because of your brain?" asks Jalaney.

Destiny nods.

"Don't suppose you'd be willing to help out a classmate," says Jalaney.

"Sure," says Destiny. "I tutor people in a bunch of subjects, including math. We have a session in the library tomorrow evening at 7:00 if you want to join us."

"That sounds great," he replies.

Class starts, cutting off their conversation. This new guy seems really nice and he's definitely cute and athletic. All pluses. *Remember your focus*, Destiny thinks.

After class, Michelle asks, "So, who was the big cute guy?"

"Oh, just a football player who is having trouble in math."

"Uh huh," says Michelle, looking at Destiny with an eyebrow raised. "And I thought you'd be too buried in your books to notice the guys."

"I'm not *noticing* him, Michelle," says Destiny. "The guy needs some help and I said I'd tutor him. That's all."

"Uh huh," says Michelle again. "Sure. Whatever you say, little sis."

The following evening, Destiny is on her way to the library. She likes to get there a little early to get prepared before any of her tutoring students show up. As she gets close to the library, she sees Jalaney, but he's not alone. There are two girls with him and they seem awfully friendly.

"Oh, Jalaney," says a blonde girl, "you shouldn't tease a girl like that."

"And why not?" asks Jalaney.

"Because you're gonna leave broken hearts all over this campus," says the other girl, tall and slim with dark curly hair.

When Destiny reaches them, the blonde girl says, "Another one?"

"Another one what?" asks Destiny, although she already knows the answer to that question.

"Oh, no," says Jalaney, putting his arm around Destiny's shoulder and smiling. "She's just my math tutor."

"Uh huh," says the dark-haired girl. She turns to Destiny, "Sugar, don't you listen to a word he says. He ain't no good."

"Uh, sure," says Destiny and the girls walk away.

"Now that ain't at all fair," calls Jalaney after the girls. Then he turns to Destiny. "Don't worry about them, Destiny. They're just messing with ya."

"Oh yeah, sure, I know," says Destiny.

"Good," says Jalaney. "Listen, after this tutoring session, do you want to go out for a bite to eat?"

"Oh, sorry," Destiny answers, "I can't tonight."

"How about another time, then?" asks Jalaney.

"Well, I don't really have a lot of free time," says Destiny. "I have a job and a lot of school work. I'm really focused on that."

"Okay," says Jalaney, "suit yourself. You know where to find me if you change your mind."

I won't change my mind, thinks Destiny. Jalaney is too much of a flirt for her liking and he's definitely not her type.

The summer has flown by, and by the end of it, Destiny is already just 18 credits away from completing her first year of college and becoming a Sophomore. She has done well in all her classes, but most of all, she has really enjoyed going to school with Michelle, whose pregnancy is starting to show. That cute little baby bump is starting to stick out and Destiny knows after the fall session Michelle will need to take some time off.

With so many courses already done and so many credits earned, Destiny feels good about where her life is headed. And with September just around the corner, the campus will really fill up with all sorts of new people. It will be exciting to meet people from other places and see what the regular school year is like.

Life is definitely good.

Part II
First Year of College

Chapter 4
New Friend

Destiny is completely in awe of college when the first week of school arrives for the fall session. College had seemed exciting in the summer session, but it couldn't possibly compare to the buzz of excitement Destiny feels as she goes to campus on her first day.

It's orientation week and all the first year students are learning their way around campus, getting their class schedules, and just generally having fun with their new-found freedom. Destiny almost wishes she weren't too busy with work. There are some really fun events going on.

The energy in the air is electric as Destiny waits in line to pick up her class schedule. "Hey there," says a voice from behind Destiny.

Destiny turns to see a girl standing behind her, long brown hair hanging over her shoulders and a colorful bag slung over one shoulder. "Hi," replies Destiny.

"Isn't this fun?" the girl says. "My name's Kresskala. What's yours?"

"I'm Destiny."

"Well, nice to meet you, Destiny," says Kresskala. "What are you taking?"

"I'm taking the Teacher Education program," replies Destiny. "What about you?"

"I'm studying to be a teacher, too! An elementary teacher."

After they get their schedules, Destiny and Kresskala walk outside. The day is sunny and warm and there are people everywhere.

"I can't believe how many people there are," says Destiny.

"I know," says Kresskala.

Just then a guy walks up to them and hands them a piece of paper. "There's a party tonight here on campus. You ladies are officially invited." He makes a gracious bow to the two of them.

Kresskala looks at the paper and then says, "Thanks! We'll be there."

"Great," the guy says before moving on to hand out more party flyers.

"You might, but I won't," says Destiny.

"No? Why not?" asks Kresskala, brushing her hair from her eyes.

"I have to work," replies Destiny.

"Oh, that's too bad," says Kresskala. "What about the rest of the week?"

"I'm pretty much booked. I work at the local grocery store. Plus I babysit for a family and I tutor part-time."

"Wow, girl! You're busy!"

"Yeah, but I'd really like to get together and do something sometime," says Destiny.

"Sounds like a great plan," says Kresskala. "Here's my number."

Destiny also gives Kresskala her phone number and they say goodbye. Destiny wants to head over to the book store before her first class starts.

Later that week, Destiny runs into Kresskala when she is on her way to the parking lot. She is done her classes for the day and Michelle is with her, her pregnant belly really starting to show.

"Hey, Destiny," says Kresskala.

"Hi, Kresskala," Destiny replies. "This is my sister, Michelle."

"Hi, Michelle," says Kresskala, sticking out her hand. "It's nice to meet you. I see you're having a baby. Destiny gets to be an aunty."

"You, too," says Michelle, shaking Kresskala's hand. "As for the baby, this is number four. Destiny's been an aunty many times over."

"My, but you are busy, aren't you? So, Destiny," says Kresskala, turning to face Destiny. "I wanted to know if you're free Saturday night to go to a movie."

Destiny thinks for a moment. "You know, I think I am free!"

"Great!" says Kresskala. "We're on then?"

"We sure are."

"OK, great," says Kresskala. "I'll call you Saturday morning to make plans."

"Sounds wonderful," says Destiny and Kresskala waves and runs off.

"It's nice to see you making some new friends," says Michelle. "You work too hard, you know. You need to get out and have some fun."

"Well, I need to work hard," says Destiny, "but I like Kresskala. It'll be fun to hang out with her."

"Well, I'm happy you're doing it," says Michelle as they reach Destiny's car. Destiny is happy, too, and very much looking forward to Saturday.

On Saturday, Destiny meets Kresskala outside the movie theater. Kresskala gives her a big hug, like they've known each other for years.

"So, what do you want to see?" asks Kresskala.

Destiny looks over the movie choices. "How about The Johnson's Family Vacation?" says Destiny.

"Awesome," says Kresskala. "That looks like a good movie."

They go in and buy their tickets and popcorn. There are only a few minutes until the movie starts, but they manage to find some good seats. They sit about halfway back from the screen and a little to the right of center.

Once they are settled into their seats, Destiny says, "So, where are you from?"

Kresskala shoves some popcorn into her mouth, chews and swallows, and says, "Sorry, I love popcorn. I live in Leesville."

"So, you have to drive here every day," Destiny says. "That must be tough."

"It's not so bad. My husband is in the military, so we have a pretty good setup there."

"Wow, my brother, Keith, is in the Air Force. I know he has a pretty good setup, too."

Kresskala seems about to respond when the lights dim and the curtains open. The movie is about to begin. Destiny settles in with her popcorn, enjoying the fact that she has such a great new friend and that she is having a fun, relaxing night out.

Chapter 5
New Job

It's the middle of October and Destiny walks through the Superstore mall. Halloween decorations are in every store window, the weather outside beginning to cool off. The summer heat has left, making way for the milder temperatures of fall.

Destiny is on her way to her first shift at the local superstore. She turned 18 at the beginning of October and now she can work anywhere. The jewelry department of the superstore is perfect because she makes more money than at the grocery store. She also makes commissions on sales and gets part-time benefits and a discount card. It seems like the perfect job.

Destiny walks into the store and looks around. There is a woman behind the counter, talking with a customer. She sees Destiny and says, "You must be Destiny. You can put your things in the back room and come on over here when you're ready."

Destiny looks around and sees the door behind the other counter. She goes in and hangs her purse and jacket on a hook.

Then she goes back out and joins the woman at the counter. The customer is on his way out of the store.

"Hi, Destiny," says the woman. "My name is Nancy River and I'll be training you."

"Hi," says Destiny, suddenly feeling very nervous. This isn't her first job, but the jewelry department is so nice, so sophisticated, compared to the grocery store.

"You've worked a cash register before?" asks Nancy.

"Yes, at the grocery store."

"Perfect," says Nancy. "Then we'll do a quick run-through of that and I'll show you the inventory."

By the end of her shift, Destiny has learned how to ring customers through, how to open the display cases to show jewelry to customers, how to take orders for jewelry repair, and how to change a watch battery.

As she leaves the store that night, she is exhausted, but exhilarated. Working at the jewelry store is going to be fantastic. She even saw a nice pair of earrings she would like to buy.

The weeks fly by and before she knows it, it's late November. Destiny is at work, cleaning the display cases, when a man's voice breaks through her thoughts.

"Hi there! You're the beautiful, short girl who was driving the big truck."

Destiny looks up to see the handsome, well-dressed man she had seen last summer when she gassed up her Pop's truck. "Oh, yes. Hi," she replies.

After a moment of silence, the man says, "What's a guy like me have to do to get some service around here?"

Destiny realizes she's just standing there staring at him and can feel her cheeks going red. She can see a twinkle in his eyes. "I... I'm sorry," she stammers. "How can I help you?"

He takes a gold watch out of his pocket. "I need a new battery for my watch. Can you replace it?"

"Yes, I can."

"Wonderful," he says. "What's your name?"

"Destiny," she says, taking his watch. As she opens it up and works on replacing the battery, the man says, "I'm Gavin."

"It's nice to meet you, Gavin," says Destiny.

"Well, it's *very* nice to meet you, Destiny," says Gavin. "I've thought about you ever since I saw you in that big truck."

Destiny can feel her heart flutter in her chest. She snaps the back of the watch back on, sets the time, and turns and hands it to Gavin.

"Now that is some fine service," he says. "How much do I owe you, pretty lady?"

"That will be $6.99."

"Well," says Gavin, handing her the money, "it was worth every penny."

Destiny rings it into the cash register and makes change for Gavin. When she hands it to him, he hands her a $20 bill.

"Oh, no, you don't owe me anything else," says Destiny.

"That's for you, darlin'," says Gavin. "For the superb service."

"Thank you," says Destiny.

"There's plenty more where that came from." Gavin winks and walks out of the store, leaving Destiny staring after him.

He is everything she could possibly want in a man. He is tall, with big brown eyes and a French man's physique. Destiny realizes he is also the first guy that has ever hit on her who actually has his own money, not his Momma's.

Destiny is in love!

When Destiny gets home from work that evening, Michelle is in the kitchen having a cup of tea with Momma. Momma takes one look at Destiny and says, "I know that look, child. You over the moon about a boy."

"No Momma, not really," Destiny replies.

"Uh huh," says Momma. "Don't you go telling me no lies, girl. I know that look."

Michelle just raises her eyebrows. She knows it, too.

"No, really," says Destiny. "There was just a nice man who gave me a big tip for changing his watch battery. That's all."

"A handsome man, no doubt," says Michelle.

"Now, not you, too, Michelle," says Destiny, getting herself a cup of tea.

"I agree with Momma," says Michelle. "That look says it all. That, child, is the look of love."

Momma nods, "Now, there's someone talkin' sense."

Destiny just smiles and sits down with her tea. *Maybe there is some sense in that,* she thinks.

Chapter 6
Friends Come and Go

It's nearing the end of March and Destiny knows exams are coming up soon. She is due to meet Kresskala so they can study together. Destiny is waiting outside the library and it isn't long before she sees Kresskala come waltzing down the hallway, books in hand.

"Hey, Destiny!" shouts Kresskala, still a good 20 feet to go before she reaches the spot where Destiny is standing.

Destiny waits until Kresskala closes the distance between them to respond. "Hi, Kresskala. You seem chipper today."

"I am!"

"Why?" asks Destiny.

"I'll tell you once we get settled in the library."

"OK," says Destiny.

As they enter the library, Kresskala asks Destiny, "So, have you seen that guy again? The $20 tipper?"

"No," replies Destiny, a note of disappointment clear in her voice.

"Darn!" says Kresskala. "Oh, well, the sea is full of fish. Or something like that." She giggles.

"I guess so, but they don't all have their own money and dress that nice. He would have been a keeper."

The girls scout out a table in a secluded corner of the library and settle in. Once their books are out on the table and opened up, Destiny says, "Okay, spill it. What's the big news? Is it good news or bad news?"

"It's both, actually," says Kresskala. "I'm moving to Japan!"

Destiny sits in silence for a moment, processing what Kresskala just said. She's going to lose her friend. That's what really stands out in her mind.

"Oh, wow, that's great," Destiny finally replies.

"Well, now, don't go getting' all excited," says Kresskala, the sarcasm oozing through her voice, despite the smile on her face and the twinkle in her eyes.

"Of course, Kresskala, it *is* great. I'm just gonna miss you, that's all."

Kresskala's smile fades a little and she sighs. "I know," she says. "To be honest, part of me is excited and the other part is terrified. I've never lived anywhere else in my life, but I knew when I married Jackson that I would get the chance to travel around. It's something that I've always wanted to do."

"Me, too," says Destiny. "To be honest, I'm a little envious."

"Oh, your time will come," says Kresskala. "One day, you'll be traveling all over the place."

"Just promise you'll keep in touch," says Destiny.

"You bet! Wouldn't have it any other way."

With that, the two friends dig into their books and start studying. Destiny knows Kresskala is right. She will travel around one day. She has seen it in her visions and knows it to be true.

The next day, Destiny runs into Josephine, a girl she takes English literature with. Josephine Jones always looked so well put together. Perfect clothes, perfect hair, perfect nails and makeup. Destiny often wondered how much time Josephine spent getting ready every morning. But despite her obvious upper-class background, she was really nice and easy to get along with. Destiny had spoken with her a few times.

"Hi, Destiny," says Josephine. Destiny is just heading down the steps outside the library, getting ready to go to work.

"Hi, Josephine," says Destiny as she stops to chat. "What are y'all doin'?" Sometimes Destiny slips into the easy slang of the south, especially when she is comfortable with someone. That's when the common southern phrases come out.

"Destiny, you southerners are a hoot," giggles Josephine. "I just love the way you talk."

Josephine is from Illinois, and she has often remarked on how southerners say things. "Just the other day, I heard a woman say she had to go make groceries. At first I couldn't figure out what on earth she was talking about, but then I realized she meant she was going grocery shopping. Honestly, I thought groceries were already made and all we have to do is buy them."

"I guess we do have some pretty silly expressions," says Destiny, feeling slightly embarrassed. "I probably never really noticed it since I grew up here."

"Well, I think it's cute," says Josephine.

Destiny doesn't feel it's cute. Josephine has reminded her that the rest of the world doesn't speak the way she does. She resolves to work extra hard to change the way she speaks so that when the time comes, she can properly communicate her message to girls around the world.

"Anyway," says Josephine, "I have to run. Bye."

"See ya," says Destiny.

Then Josephine stops and turns to face Destiny. "Would you like to come driving with me and some friends of mine this weekend? We are going to go out on Sunday afternoon and see what there is to see."

Destiny is excited to be invited. "Sure, I'd love that."

"Okay, great," says Josephine. "I'll pick you up at your house at 1:00 Sunday afternoon."

"I'll be ready," says Destiny and she gives Josephine her address.

Sunday arrives and Josephine shows up promptly at 1:00. She pulls up into the end of Destiny's driveway in a great big Cadillac Deville. All of a sudden, Destiny feels slightly embarrassed by her tiny middle class house. *Oh well*, thinks Destiny, *she's here now so I might as well make the best of it.*

Destiny can see two other girls in the back seat of the car as she walks up to it. Josephine waves to her, gesturing for her to sit in the front seat. Destiny gets in and Josephine says, "Hey, Destiny. I'm so glad you could join us. This is Jamie Oliver and Debbie Turnkey."

Each of the girls in the back wave in turn and say, "Hi, Destiny."

"Hi," says Destiny. "It's nice to meet you."

The interior of the car is amazing. Comfortable leather seats and automatic everything. *I could definitely get used to this level of luxury*, thinks Destiny as she sinks into the seat. Although, she knows deep down that she wouldn't trade her Ford Contour for anything. It is her first car and she bought it with her own money.

Josephine drives out of town and heads along Highway 6 toward Natchitoches. Even though it was a drive Destiny did daily to and from school, it somehow felt different in Josephine's Cadillac.

The girls chat about so many things as they drive. Everyone is so nice and Destiny relaxes and really enjoys their company. Soon, Josephine says, "So, Destiny, have you ever thought of joining a sorority?"

"Not really," replies Destiny.

"Oh, wow, you totally should," says Josephine.

"We all belong to the Greek Life Sorority," says Debbie. "It's fantastic!"

"I guess I can think about it," says Destiny. "I'm just so busy with school and work, I'm not sure I'd have the time."

"Well, you *should* think about it," says Josephine. "It's a blast."

"Okay, I will," says Destiny. The truth is Destiny isn't so sure she wants to take the pledge for a sorority. She has heard stories about initiation and they scare her. She'll stick with the 'too busy' excuse. After all, it's the truth.

The rest of the drive is wonderful. They stop off at a diner and have a bite to eat and some guys flirt with them. This sends them into fits of giggles and gives them something new to talk about on the drive home. All in all, Destiny has a great afternoon and is glad to have new friends.

Part III
Second Year of College

Chapter 7
Drake

It's Saturday afternoon and Destiny is at the grocery store, running an errand for Momma. The summer flew by and Destiny's second year of college has started. She is thrilled to be back at school full-time, but things are busier than ever. After her errand for Momma, Destiny has to go to work at the Jewelry store. Then she has an evening of studying ahead of her.

Destiny is in the baking aisle when she feels a tap on her shoulder. She turns around to find Drake standing there.

"Hi, Destiny," he says.

"Hi, Drake."

"How have you been doing?" asks Drake.

"Oh, I'm just fine," says Destiny. "Just fine. And you?"

"I've been good," says Drake. "I'm an assistant manager, now."

"That's great, Drake! Congratulations!"

"Listen, Destiny. The truth is I miss you. I've missed you ever since you stopped working here. Ever since I messed up."

"Uh, okay," says Destiny, feeling awkward and not knowing what to say.

"Would you be willing to go out on a date with me?" Drake asks.

Destiny is stunned. She certainly wasn't expecting this during her shopping trip. She looks at Drake and considers. He has done well at work, getting a promotion and all, and he looks and acts more mature. He even admitted to screwing up before. Maybe he deserves a second chance.

"Sure, I would like that, Drake," says Destiny.

"Oh, that's super, Destiny," says Drake. "Are you free for dinner this evening?"

"Yeah, I can meet you after I get off work at 6:00."

"Okay, meet me here and we'll find somewhere nice," says Drake.

"Sure, sounds great," says Destiny and Drake goes back to work while she finishes her shopping. Destiny is excited. This might just turn out okay.

Destiny picks a French fry off of Drake's plate and dips it in the ketchup. She has been seeing him for five weeks now and everything has gone so well that sometimes she can hardly believe it. Drake has been nothing but a perfect gentleman.

"So, Destiny Unique," says Drake, "What do you want to do after dinner?"

"What did you just call me?"

Drake pauses before speaking. "Well now, I called you Destiny."

"No," says Destiny, shaking her head. "You called me Destiny Unique. Who is Destiny Unique?"

"Well, um..." Drake stumbles for the words. "You see, I was just calling you Destiny unique, you know, because you're so unique."

"Really?" says Destiny. "That's a pretty lame lie, Drake."

"I'm telling you the truth," says Drake. "Honest."

But Drake will not look her in the eye. "You've been cheating on me!" says Destiny, standing up and taking out her car keys.

"No, Destiny, honey. You're the only one I want."

Destiny doesn't even let him gone on with his lying. Her gut tells her he's been cheating on her. "See you around, Drake," she says and she walks out of the diner.

Destiny pulls into her driveway and gets out of her car, slamming the door far too hard. Why can't she find a good guy? Is it really that hard to do?

She goes into the house and slips off her shoes. On her way through the living room she hears Michelle shout from the kitchen. "Hey, sweetie. Come on in here and say hi."

Destiny goes into the kitchen and sees Michelle fixing her a cup of tea. "I thought you might want one."

"I guess so," says Destiny.

"Oh now, I know that look, honey," says Michelle as she sets Destiny's tea on the table and takes a seat. "What happened? Did that Drake guy treat you wrong?"

Destiny didn't answer right away and Michelle just shook her head. But she stayed silent, waiting until Destiny was ready to talk.

"He called me Destiny Unique."

"What, now?" asks Michelle. "He called you another girl's name?"

"Yeah," says Destiny, wrapping her hands around her warm cup of tea. "I just don't get it, sis. Why can't I find a decent guy? I mean look at you? You found Flintstone when you were my age, younger even, and he's stuck by you. Why can't I find someone like that?"

Michelle's husband's name is Earl Flintstone Vines, but everyone in town just calls him Flintstone.

Michelle just looks at Destiny and takes her hand. "Now you listen here, Linelle Destiny. That Drake is no good and never has been. I never could understand why you gave him another chance, but now that's water under the bridge."

Destiny nods, tears coming to her eyes.

Michelle continues, "I know you can and will do better than him, now, you hear? Much better. You have your own Flintstone out there waiting for you and he's gonna treat you right. You'll find him when the time is right and not a moment sooner."

Destiny nods again and Michelle reaches up and wipes Destiny's tears away.

"Besides," says Michelle, "that big old brain of yours is too busy with school to be thinking about boys. You need to focus on your studies, girl!"

That's just what Grandma Lucy Belle told Destiny and she knows this is the right advice.

"Thanks, Michelle," says Destiny, sipping her tea. She vows to put Drake behind her and put her mind where it needs to be, starting with studying tonight. After she finishes her tea.

Chapter 8
Gavin

It's been a week since Destiny broke up with Drake. She's had a hard time not feeling sorry for herself, but she has decided to dive into her school work and that has certainly helped. Today, Destiny is at work. It's Saturday afternoon and the jewelry store has been busy. Probably people getting an early jump on their holiday shopping.

Destiny finishes up with a customer and starts cleaning the jewelry cases when someone says, "Hi there."

Destiny looks up to see Gavin standing in front of her. "Oh. Hi, Gavin. What can I do for you today? Do you need your watch battery changed again?"

"What you can do for me is go out on a date with me," says Gavin.

Destiny can feel her cheeks turning red. "Oh, well... I...," stammers Destiny.

"I just keep thinking of you," says Gavin. "I'd really like to get to know you better. Can I pick you up and take you to dinner tonight?"

Destiny finally finds her voice. "Yes, I'd like that, Gavin."

"Great," says Gavin and Destiny gives him her address. "I'll pick you up at 7:00."

"Okay, see you then," says Destiny.

Gavin winks at her and walks out of the store. Destiny sighs and smiles to herself. She has always been interested in Gavin, but she didn't know he was interested in her. Plus, Gavin has to be better than Drake ever was.

Destiny is waiting on her doorstep when Gavin arrives promptly at 7:00. Destiny takes a deep breath before she walks down the steps and over to the car.

Gavin gets out and opens the door for her. "How are you this evening, Destiny?" he asks. It feels strange to have a man act like such a gentleman.

Gavin's car is beautiful! It's a white Mitsubishi Galant and the interior is warm, the color of peanut butter and caramel. The leather seats are plush and comfortable, the dash board elegant.

When Gavin gets into the car, he reaches in the back and hands Destiny a beautiful bouquet of candy cane red roses. "Oh, my," says Destiny, nearly speechless. No man has ever given her flowers before. "Thank you, Gavin. They're beautiful!"

"Well, I like beautiful things," he replies, staring into her eyes. "Do you like seafood?"

"Yes."

"Great," says Gavin. "I know the perfect restaurant."

"Once they arrive at the restaurant, have been seated, and their meals ordered, Destiny sips her virgin pia colada and they chat.

"So, tell me what you are taking at school," says Gavin.

"I'm studying teacher education because I really enjoy teaching people. You know, really working with them," Destiny replies.

"I bet you're a great teacher."

"I don't know," says Destiny. "I really love it though. I've been tutoring people since high school."

"Wow, I'm not sure I could pull that off, trying to teach something to someone else," says Gavin. "I like working on my own."

Destiny smiles, "Well, I don't find it hard."

"I bet you're a natural."

"What about you?" asks Destiny. "What do you do?"

"I work at Boise Cascade. We manufacture a lot of wood products, mostly for use as building materials."

"That sounds exciting," says Destiny.

"Yeah, I guess so," says Gavin. "It pays the bills, anyway."

As their food is delivered, Destiny thinks Gavin's job must do more than just pay the bills. He seems to have a very lavish lifestyle. He has a fabulous car and very nice clothes. He has given her long-stemmed roses and taken her out to a really nice restaurant.

As they eat, they chat about various things, like what's happening around town and about their childhoods. Destiny feels very content. Maybe Gavin is the one for her. She sure hopes so.

Destiny gets home from school on a Monday afternoon. She has had a wonderful week. Despite being busy, she has been out with Gavin three more times. When she walks through the door she spies a letter at the top of the pile of mail. It's addressed to her.

Excitement rises in Destiny as she picks up the letter. She just loves getting mail. Maybe it's from Kresskala. Destiny hasn't heard from her in a while. But when Destiny looks closely at the return address on the envelope she sees it's from Alvin.

Destiny's Momma calls from the kitchen, "That you, Destiny?"

"Yes, Momma."

"Good," Momma says, "I need you help in here gettin' dinner ready."

"Okay, Momma," Destiny calls back. "I'm just gonna put my things away and I'll be right in."

Destiny goes to her room and sits on her bed for a moment, staring at the letter. She doesn't know what to do. She hasn't heard from Alvin in a long time. The return address is in Paris and she really wants to know what he's doing there.

But then there's Gavin. Destiny is seeing him now and she feels like it would be a betrayal if she opened Alvin's letter. Maybe she shouldn't.

Destiny takes the letter and tucks it into her journal, where it will be safe. Perhaps a better time to read the letter will come.

Destiny heads to the kitchen to help with dinner.

Chapter 9
Alvin

Destiny is trying to study, but it's difficult to focus. It's been difficult to focus on anything for the past week, ever since she received Alvin's letter in the mail. It's hardest of all when she's at home, studying in her room, with the letter tucked into her journal that is lying on the desk, just a foot away from her. She can see the envelope sticking out of the top of the journal.

Destiny decides she simply can't take it any longer. She reaches over and grabs her journal, pulling the letter out of it. Then she sits there and stares at it for what must be a minute or two before she sticks her thumb under the edge of the sealed flap and rips open the envelope.

Destiny reads the letter through. He tells her how much fun he is having in France, where he is competing for the world title in the 400s. *Good for him*, Destiny thinks.

Then he says, "I really miss you, Destiny. I think about you every day and I have realized how very important you are to me. I really hope we can see each other again soon, pick up

where we left off, maybe start the relationship I wish we had started before."

After Destiny finishes reading Alvin's letter, she realizes deep in her heart that she feels the same way about him as he feels about her. She really wishes she had the chance to explore a relationship with Alvin, but he's so far away, and besides, she's with Gavin now and she's got something good going with him. She doesn't want to mess that up.

She tucks Alvin's letter away again and turns back to her studying. At least now she feels more content knowing what the letter said.

A couple of weeks later, Destiny is waiting for Gavin at the diner. It's Friday night and he was supposed to meet her at 6:00. She looks at her watch. It's nearly 7:00 and he hasn't shown up yet. Destiny is beginning to worry about him. He's always on time.

Destiny hears the bell on the door jingle and looks over expectantly, hoping to see Gavin come in. It's not him, but it is a guy she has seen Gavin talking to before. Maybe he knows something about why Gavin hasn't come by yet.

She decides to go and ask him if he's seen Gavin. She approaches him as he sits at the counter, waiting for a cup of coffee. "Excuse me," says Destiny. "You're a friend of Gavin's, right?"

"Yeah, sugar, that's right," he answers, his black leather jacket squeaking a bit as he turns to face her.

"Well," Destiny continues, "he was supposed to meet me here an hour ago and he's never late. Do you happen to know where he might be or why he's so late?"

Gavin's buddy looks Destiny up and down and then says, "Oh yeah, he got busted. He's in jail tonight, honey, so he won't be meeting you."

Destiny is shocked and a little nervous. Gavin in jail? "But what was Gavin busted for? I don't understand," she says to Gavin's buddy.

"You tellin' me you don't know what Gavin's got going on?"

"No, I don't," says Destiny.

"Huh," he says. "How'd Gavin ever hook up with you, anyway? Have a seat and tell me all about it. You can hang with me if you want." He pats the seat next to him, a creepy looking smile crossing his face.

"Uh, no, but thanks," Destiny says. "I really wasn't meeting him for long tonight, anyway. I have studying to do." With that she turns and walks toward the door.

"Suit yourself," says Gavin's buddy, just before the door shuts behind her and cuts off the sound of his voice.

Destiny sits in her car for a while, thinking about what Gavin's friend said. What on earth could have made it so Gavin would get arrested? It obviously isn't anything good, but now she knows why he didn't show up. It's pretty tough to keep a date when you're in jail.

Destiny thinks about Gavin's lavish lifestyle, his fancy car and fine clothes. She thinks about how he always showers her with flowers, expensive dinners, and nice gifts. She always wondered how he could afford such luxury on the salary he makes at the wood mill. Now she is convinced he's earning it another way, a way she wants no part of.

Destiny starts her car and pulls out of the parking lot. She has a very bad vibe about Gavin and the situation he's mixed up in. She decides that's it, she's done with him. She has a good life ahead of her with plenty of success and a goal of helping others. She doesn't want anything to mess that up and no guy is worth that sort of risk. Destiny goes home and refocuses her sights on what really matters.

Chapter 10
Epilogue

Destiny spends the next few days after ending her relationship with Gavin mechanically going about her responsibilities. She feels like all the fire has gone out of her and once again she wonders why she can't find the right man for her. Can it really be that difficult?

She also keeps thinking about Alvin, perhaps the one guy she's known who would be right for her and he's half a world away from her. One evening, when Destiny finishes her studying for the day, she pulls out Alvin's letter. She curls up on her bed and opens the letter, reading it again.

Alvin clearly has strong feelings for her and she knows she has those feelings for him. She decides it's time to write back to him. Now that she is not in a relationship with anyone, she doesn't feel guilty about keeping in touch with Alvin.

In her letter, Destiny apologizes for taking so long to get back to him. She tells Alvin how envious she is that he has been in France and asks him how it is there and how the competition went. Then she tells him about her studies, her job at the

jewelry store, and how busy she is here at home. She decides it's best not to tell him about her relationship with Gavin, at least not right now.

She finishes the letter by telling him that she also misses him and that she also has strong feelings for him. She asks him when he might be coming back this way. Then she signs off and gets the letter ready to mail, meticulously printing the address on the envelope, writing her return address, and placing a stamp on it. She will drop it in the mailbox first thing in the morning.

With a sigh, Destiny places the letter on her desk and gets ready for bed, feeling a mix of sadness and fondness for Alvin.

That night, Destiny has a dream. She is standing on a beach in a beautiful white dress. The dress is subtle and strapless, her veil blowing in the ocean breeze. She is standing under a white canopy, which shades her from the hot sun. Beside her stands Alvin, staring into her eyes, and she is surrounded by their close friends and family, all seated in chairs, watching the happy couple.

It's her wedding, marrying Alvin in a simple ceremony on a beach in Jamaica. Everything is perfect and she adores him. She can see that he also adores her. There is someone officiating, pronouncing them husband and wife. He says, "You may kiss the bride."

Destiny wakes with a start. She can still feel Alvin's presence, the dream was so vivid. What a wonderful dream! She feels an incredible amount of love for Alvin, more than she has ever felt for anyone, but he is so far away. She has no idea when she will see him again, if ever.

Destiny's heart almost aches for Alvin, but she knows it's for the best. If he was here and she could have a relationship with him, it would be all-consuming and she has committed to her education. It would be so difficult to juggle both and she fears her studies would suffer.

Still, she wishes Alvin were here so she could see him, even for just a little while. She gives her head a shake, and says to herself, "Linelle Destiny, you know it's for the best right now. Keep your head on straight and don't go mooning after no boy."

Despite this pep talk and the fact that she knows it's for the best, Destiny has a hard time getting back to sleep because all she can think of is Alvin.

About the Author

Alicia Linelle Holland was born and raised in Many, Louisiana and got her middle name after her mother, Vera Linelle. When Alicia was in middle school, she started the Secret Sister Club that you read about in the Linelle Destiny Book Series. Alicia Holland has been working towards bringing back the Secret Sister Club as she embarks upon quite an interesting life and spiritual journey. At age 26, she earned her Doctorate in Education so that she can be in a position to help others believe in themselves and go far. At age 31, Dr. Alicia Holland opened a Not for Profit, Alise Spiritual Healing & Wellness Center and was officially ordained as a Minister. As a Transformational Life Coach, Professor, Author, Speaker, and Minister, Dr. Holland travels the World sharing her message: "You are Loved, You are Valued, and You are Competent.

Dr. Alicia Holland has two beautiful daughters, ages 7 and 9, who travels the World with her and are active participants in the Secret Sister Club Mentoring Program. She and her family resides in Austin, Texas and are currently looking for a new puppy.

Dr. Holland is available for speaking engagements and can be reached at support@thesecretsistersclub.com or support@iglobaleducation.com.